THE ZOO THAT GREW

Illustrated by Lisl Stich
Text by James Krüss
Adapted by Sarah Keyser

Platt & Munk Publishers/New York

2.79

First published in Germany with the title *Ich War So Gerne Zoodirektor*
by Boje-Verlag, Stuttgart. Original German text and illustrations
© 1968 by Boje-Verlag, Stuttgart. All rights reserved.
Library of Congress Catalog Card Number 77-114667
Printed in Belgium

What would *you* do if your father had a huge farm and one day he gave it all to you? Well, that's just what happened to Harry. And the first thing Harry did was to invite his friends over — Pierre the Polar Bear, Maurice the Monkey and Hilda the Hippo.

The next day Hilda the Hippo brought her baby with her and two men from the newspaper came to take pictures. Peter Penguin brought carrots, apples, pears and turnips for the baby and Harry was so happy that right then and there he decided to make the farm into a *zoo*.

Soon everybody knew about Harry's zoo and wanted to live there. The Wolf Family came first and Harry built them a large round house. Then Reginald Rhinoceros lumbered by and Harry gave him the field next door. Harry wanted his new friends to have soft beds so he brought back bales and bales of hay.

The zoo grew and grew. Peter Penguin's family —all twenty-one of them—came down from the North Pole. Archibald the Alligator travelled all the way from China. They quickly became friends and made their home in the bright sunshine right next to the monkey house.

The good news about Harry's zoo travelled all over. The penguins told their friends what a happy place it was. Soon four pairs of brightly-colored birds flew in and Harry built them a roomy house with beautiful flowers and trees so they, too, would feel at home.

Harry was busy every minute. He brushed Hilda's teeth three times a day and just before dinner he scrubbed George the Giraffe from head to toe. That was a tall job and Harry had to get a tall ladder to do it right.

Harry wanted to make his zoo the biggest and the best in the whole world. So he went to the city to see how a really big zoo was run. It was not at all what he expected. Noisy boys were teasing the animals, so Harry helped the zookeeper shoo them out the gate.

Harry saw other children throwing rocks at the bears while some of the grown-ups were *laughing*!! At that moment, Harry made up his mind that this would never happen in his zoo.

Animals and people should be friendly. So Harry invited them all together and told them that everyone would be happier if they were nice to each other.

Every night when Harry fell asleep, he dreamed of new ways to make his zoo bigger and better. Oh, there were so many things he wanted to do — like building a rock garden and planting trees and making a pond for the fish.

Harry's zoo grew and grew. And all the animals were kind to each other. The dog and the cat became the best of friends, the wolf played with the sheep, the eagle baby-sat for the little pigeons and the owl played ball with the mouse.

When everybody was happily settled in their new homes, Harry built a bright red brick wall around the zoo. But he kept the wall low so that the animals could look out and the people could look in and see how Harry's zoo had grown to be the friendliest place in the whole world.